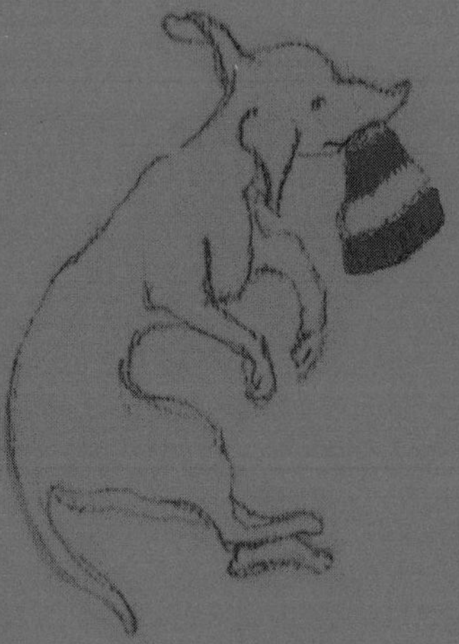

se return / renew by date sho

KU-759-345

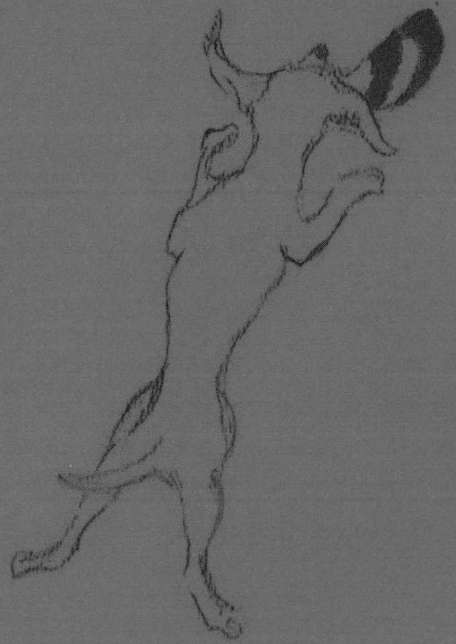

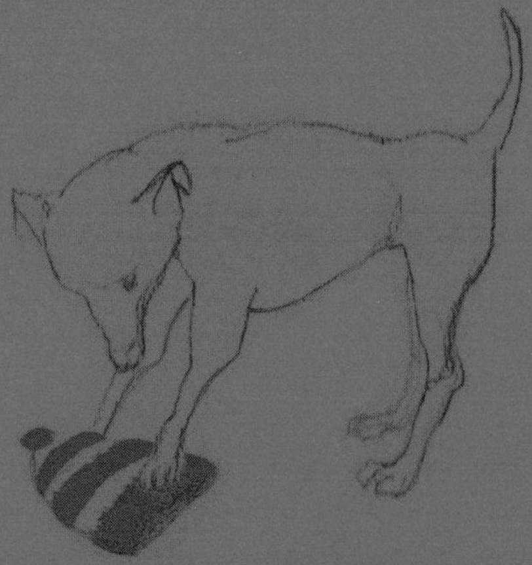

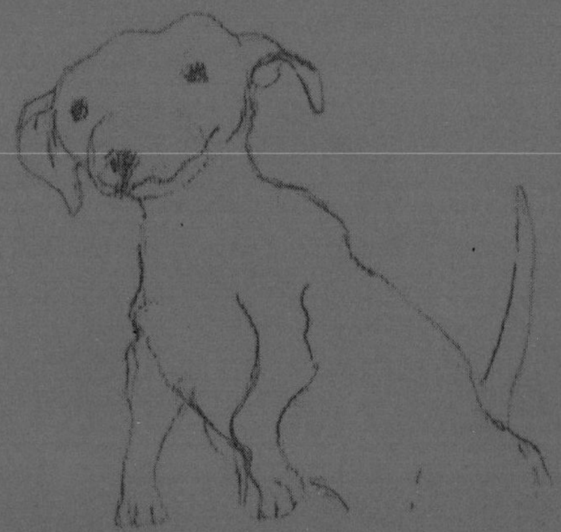

KATE PRENDERGAST

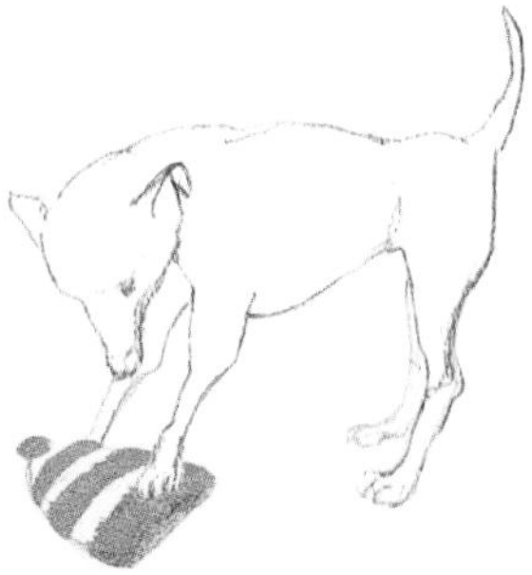

DOG ON A TRAIN

Old Barn Books

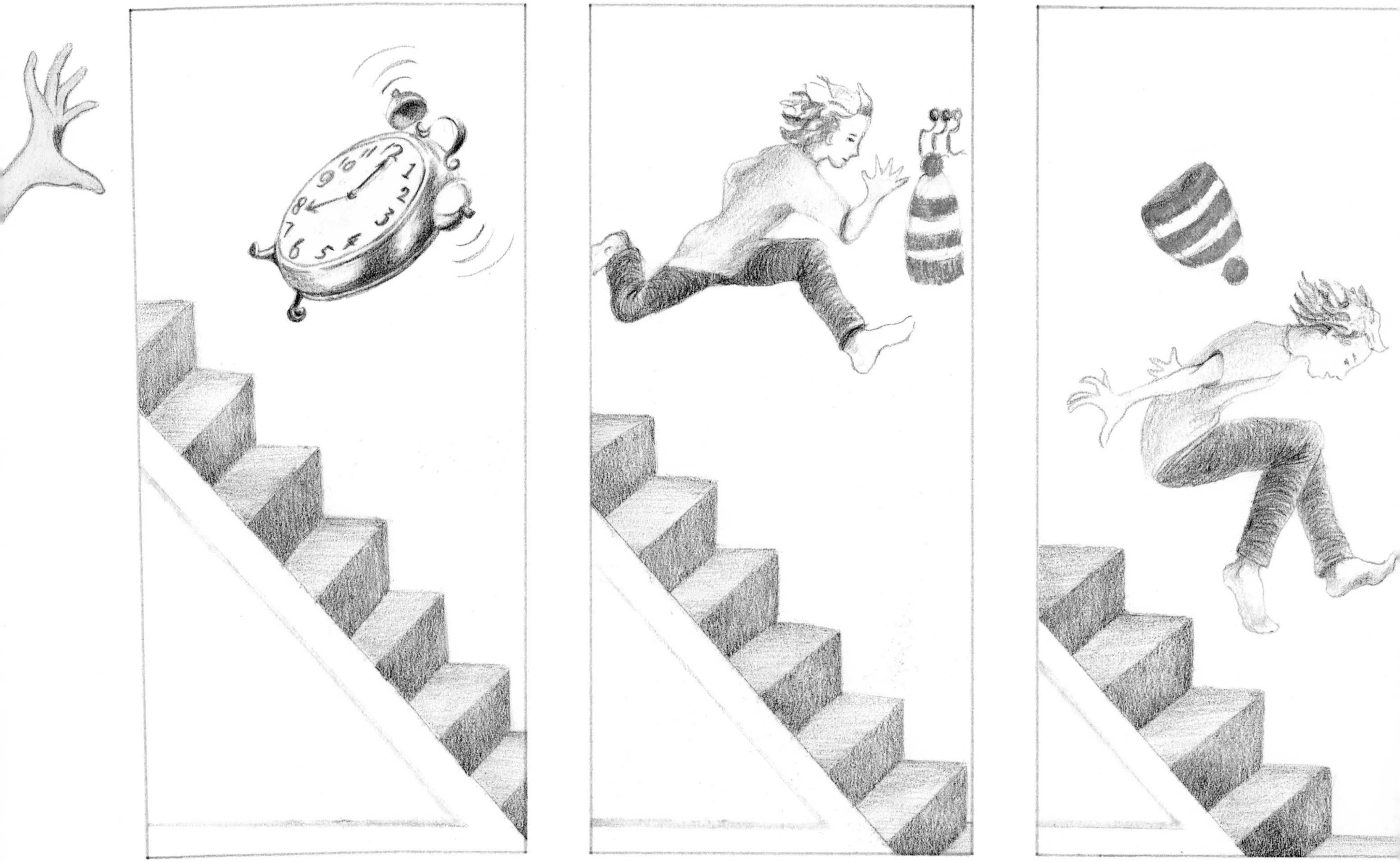

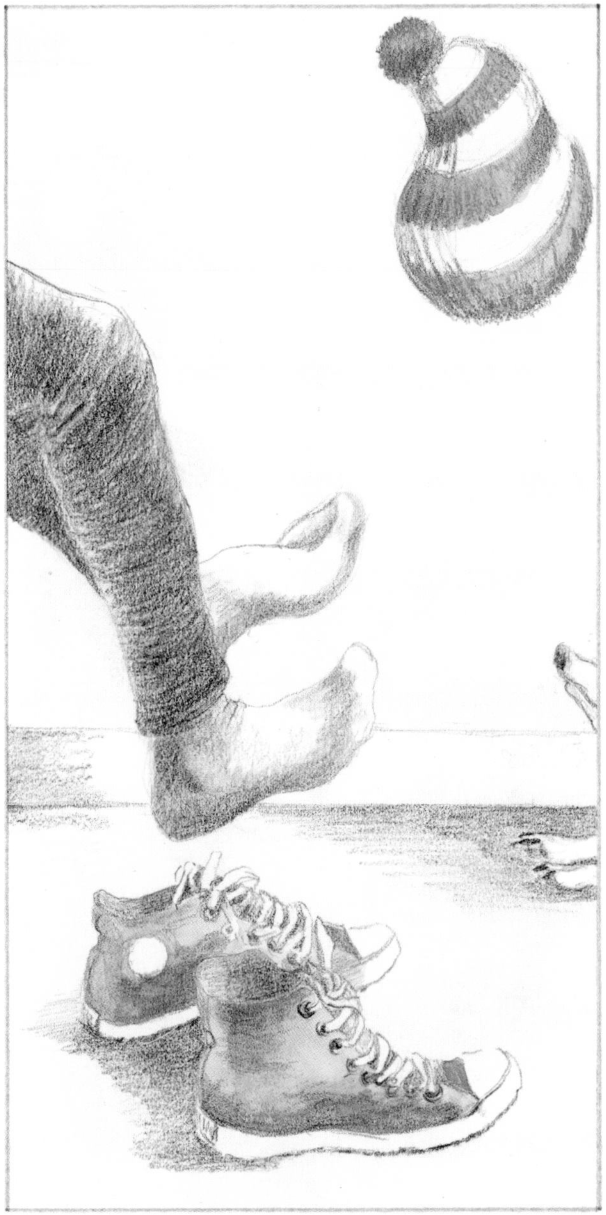
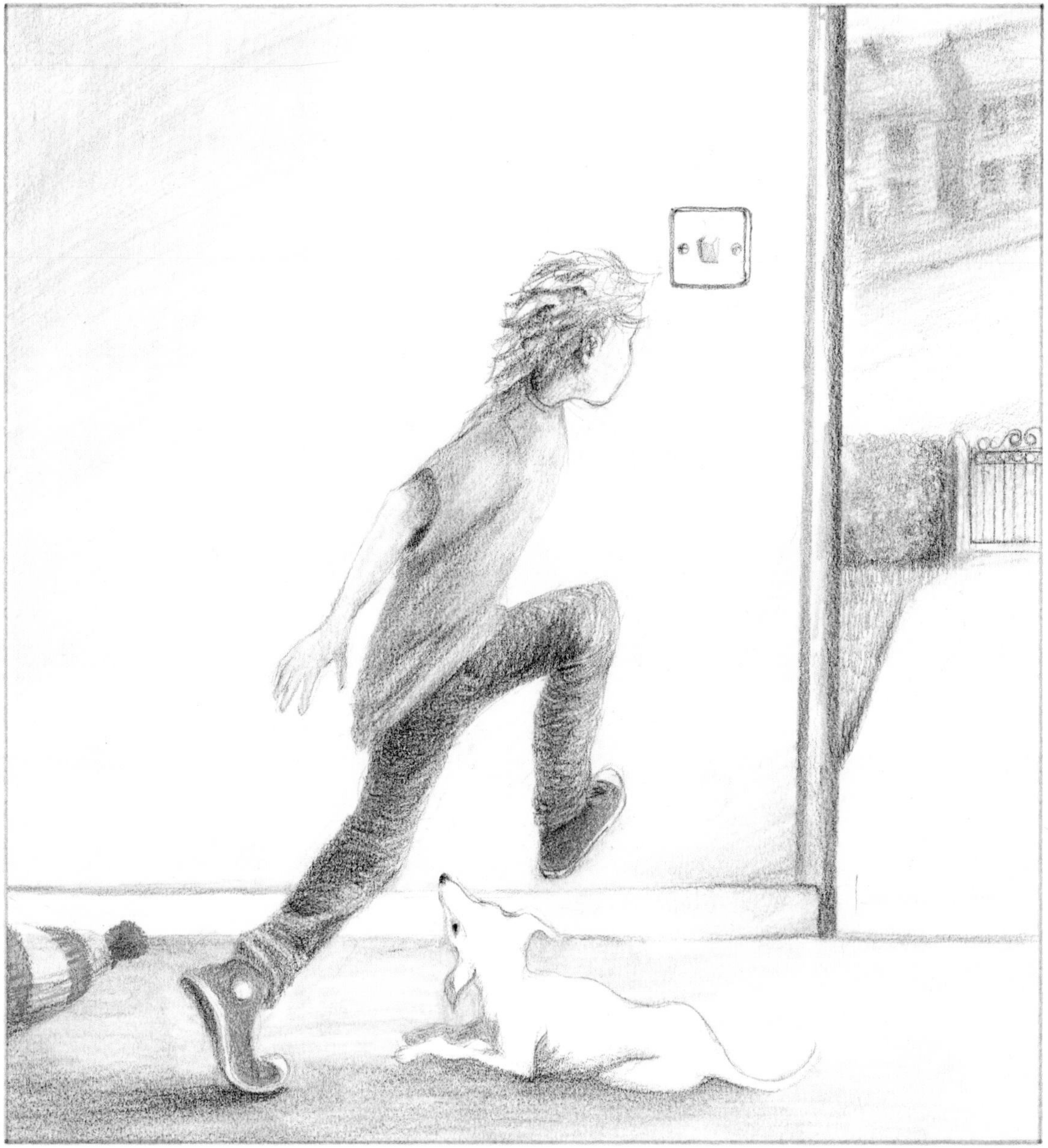

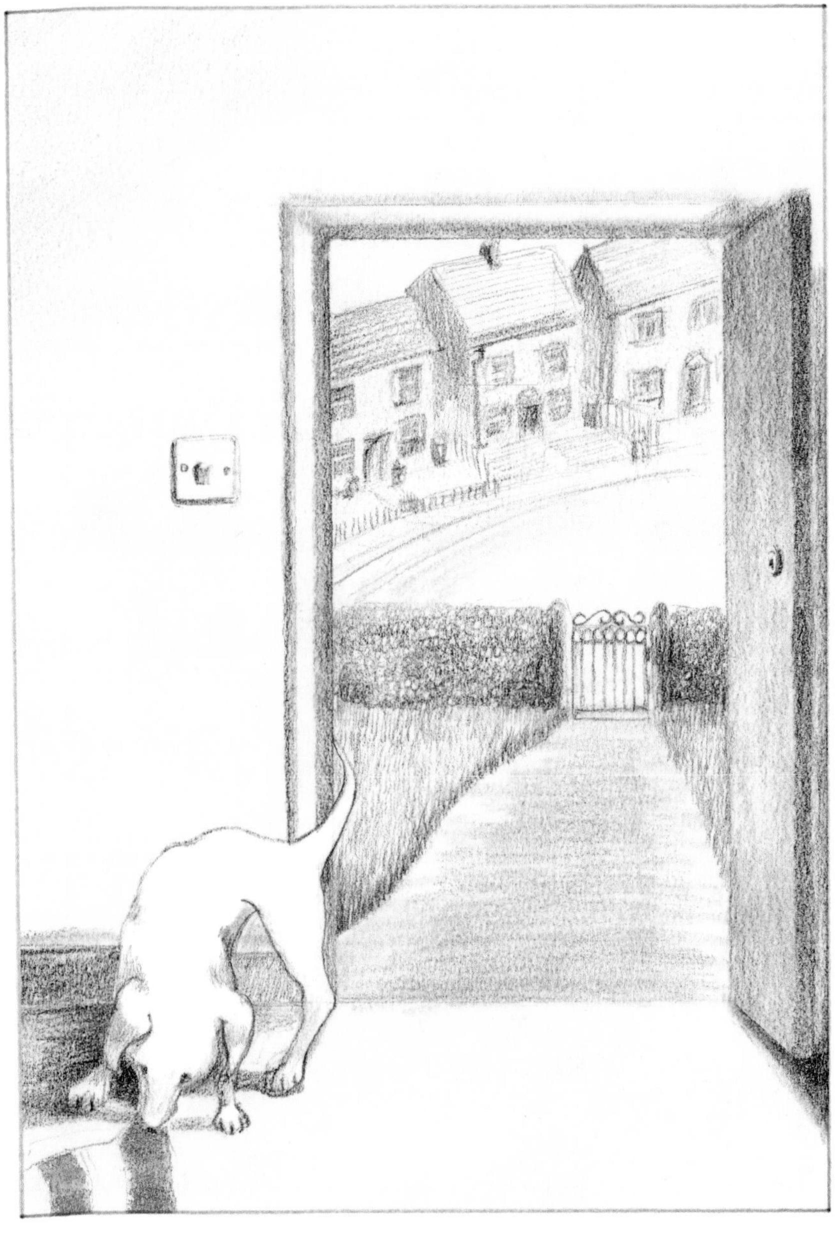

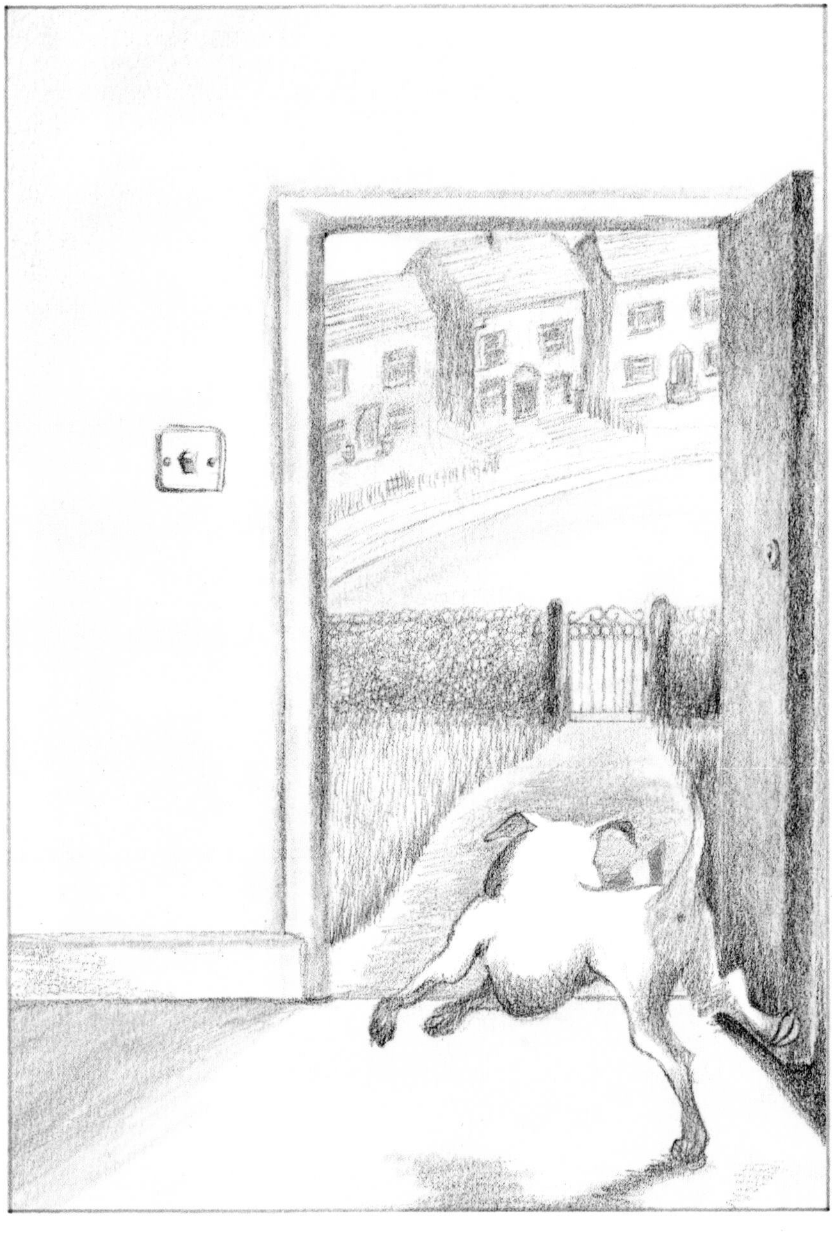

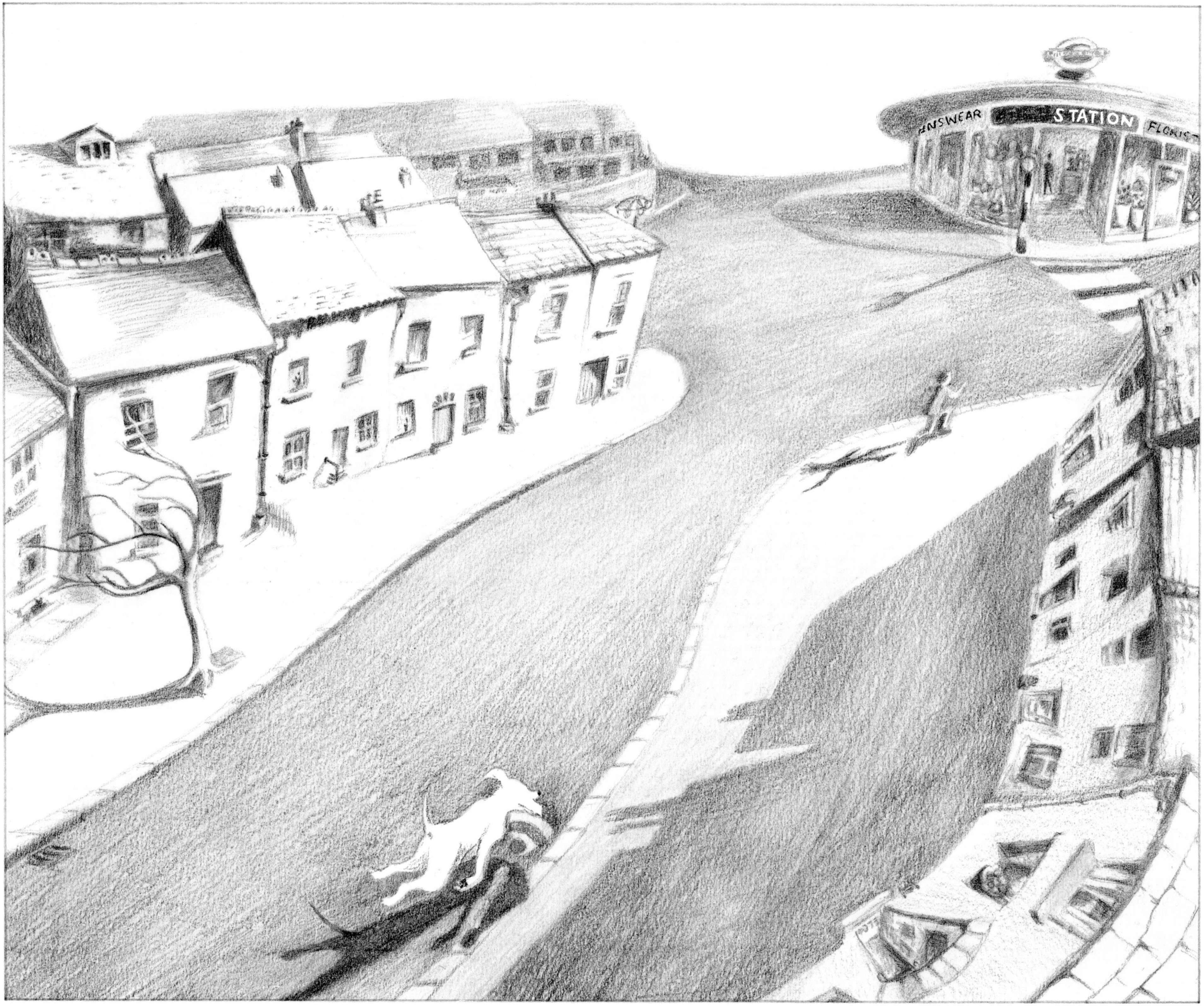
STATION

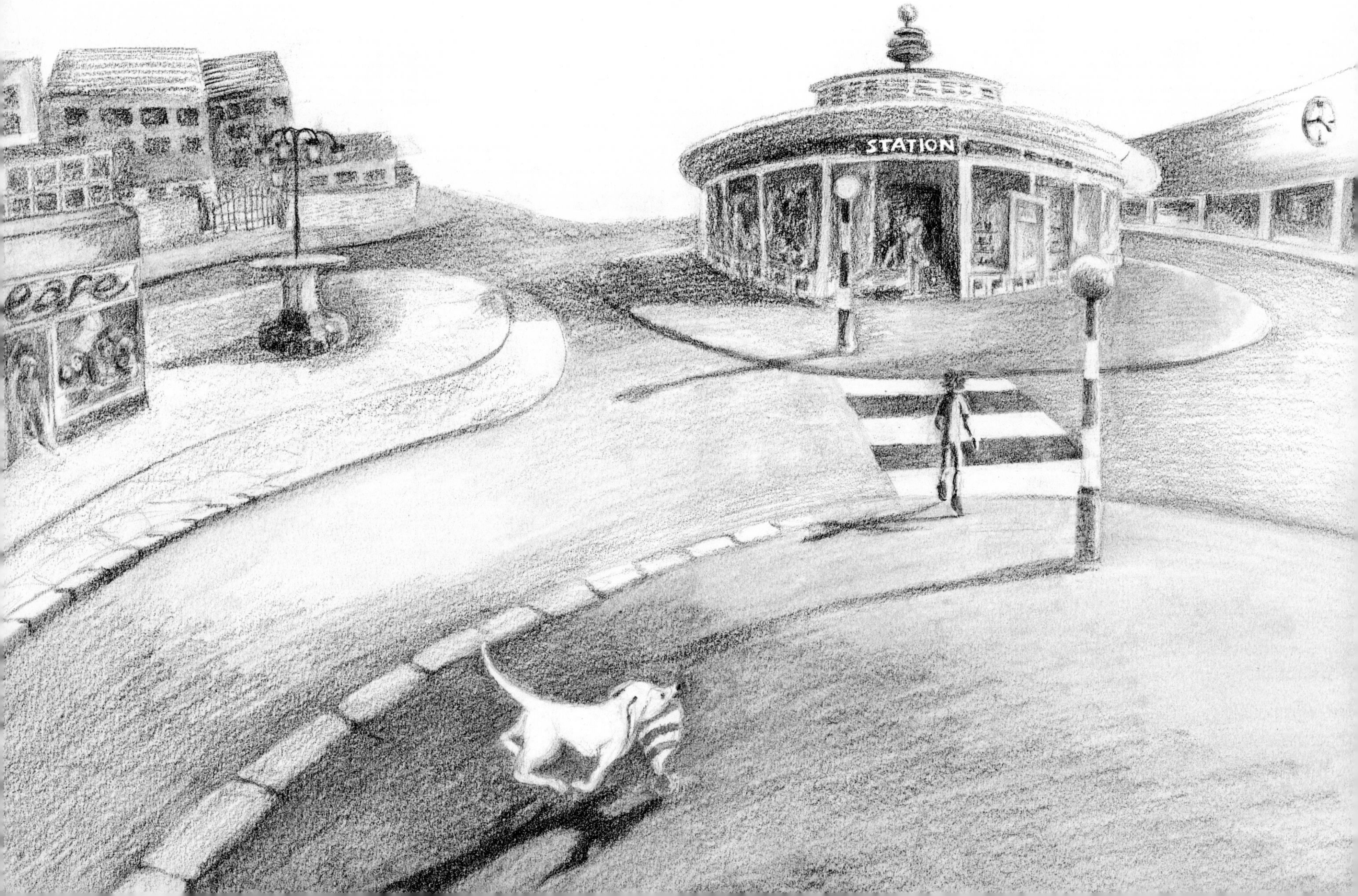
STATION
cafe

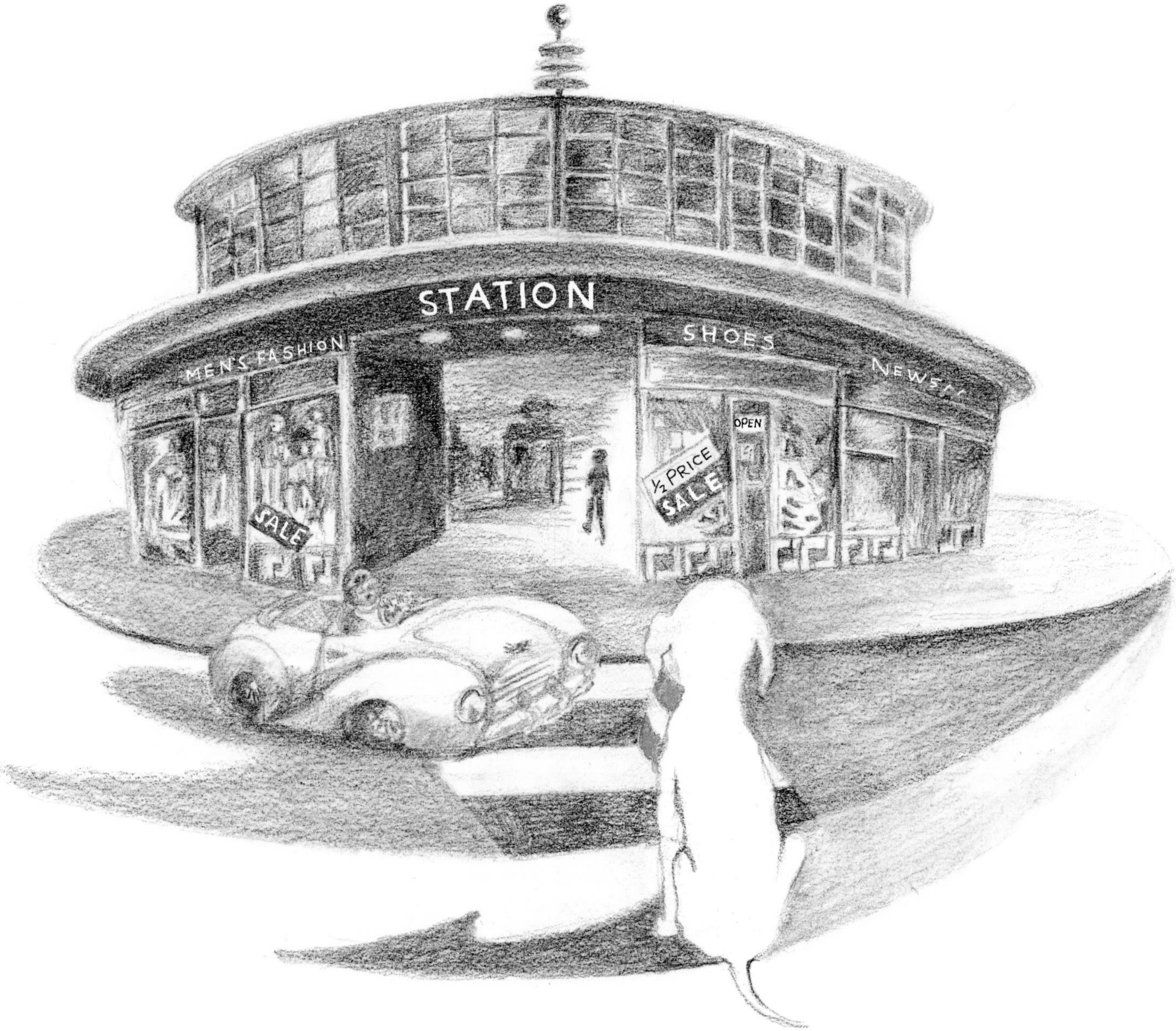
STATION
MENS FASHION
SHOES
OPEN
SALE
½ PRICE SALE

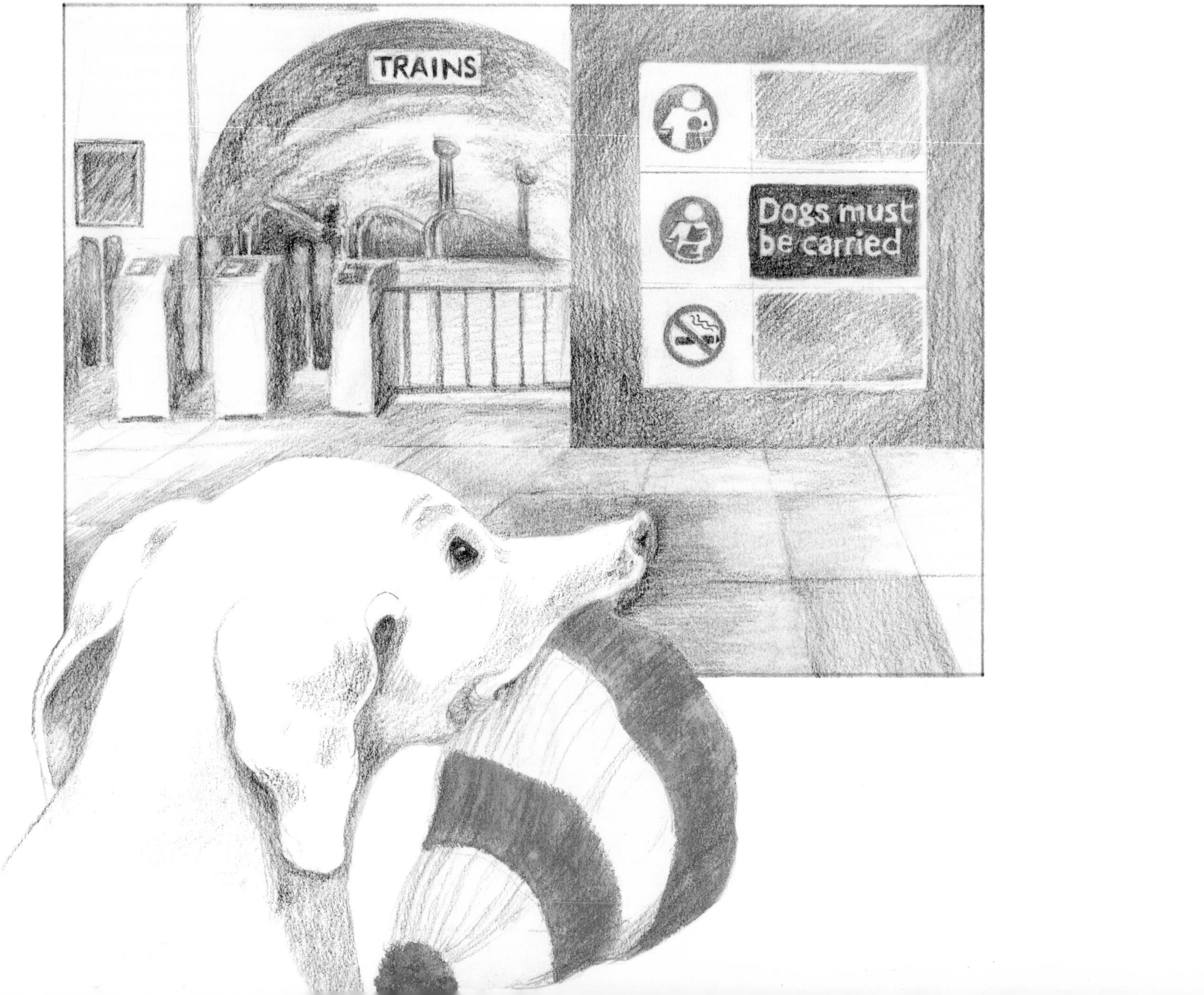
TRAINS
Dogs must be carried

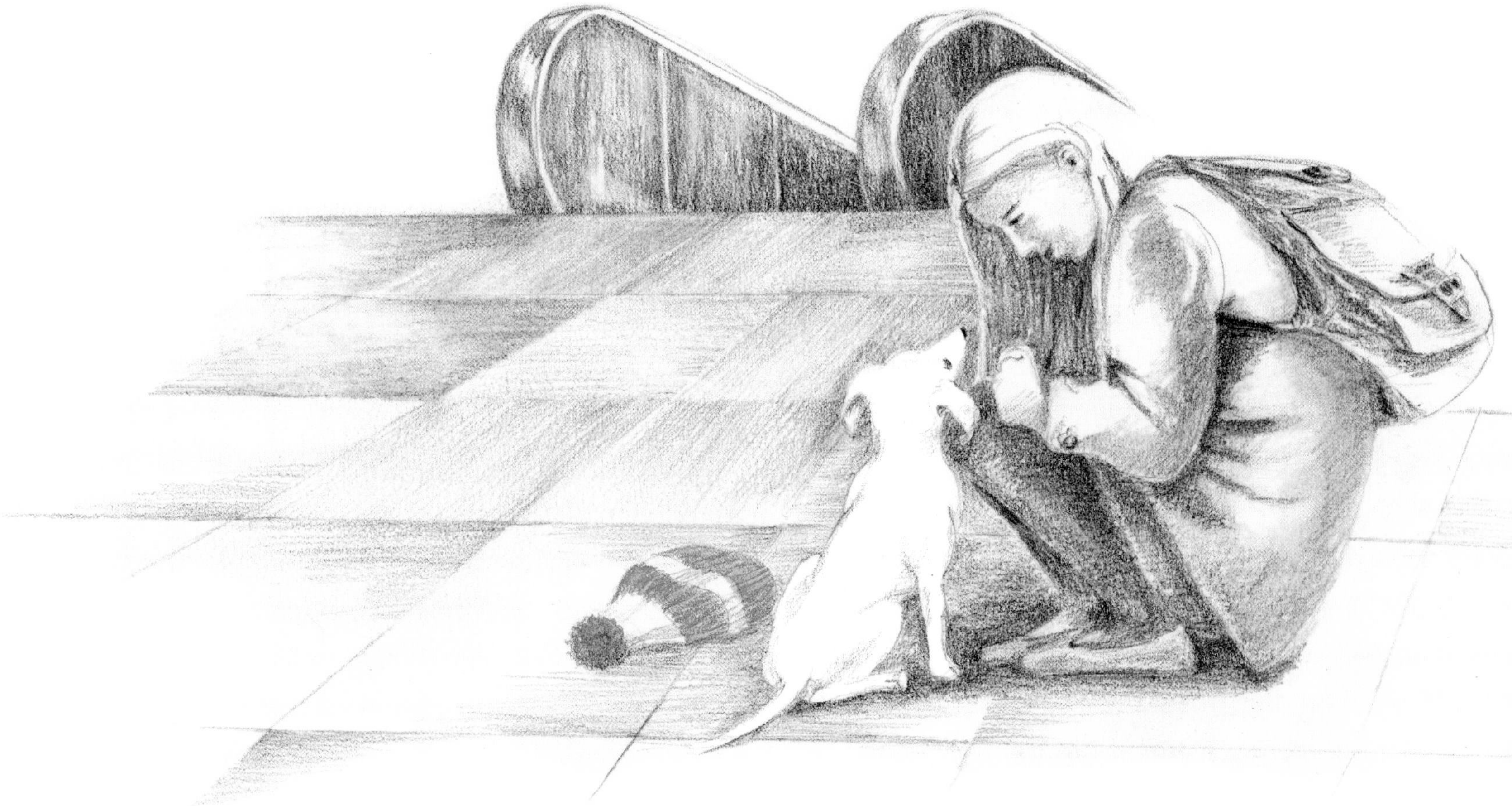

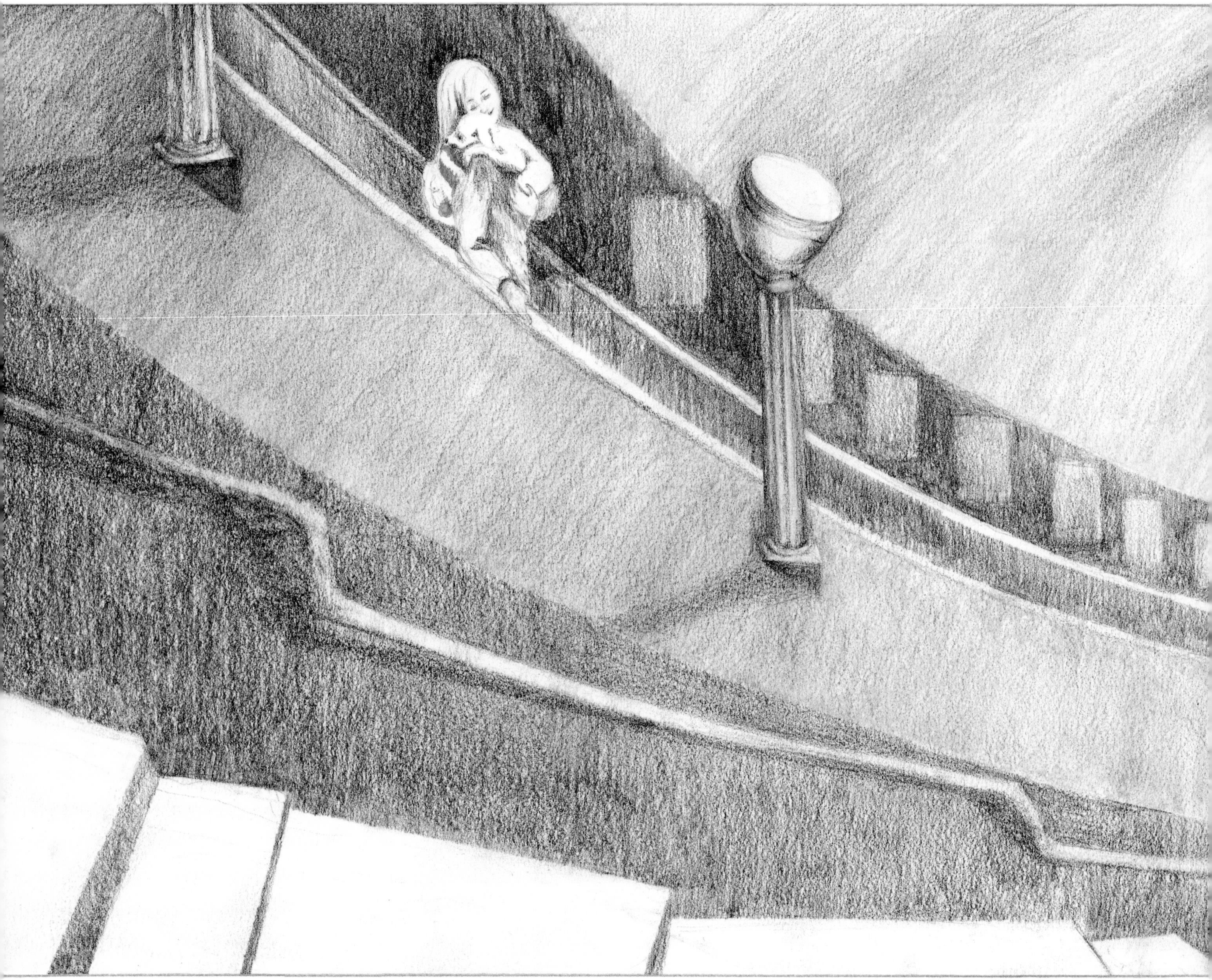

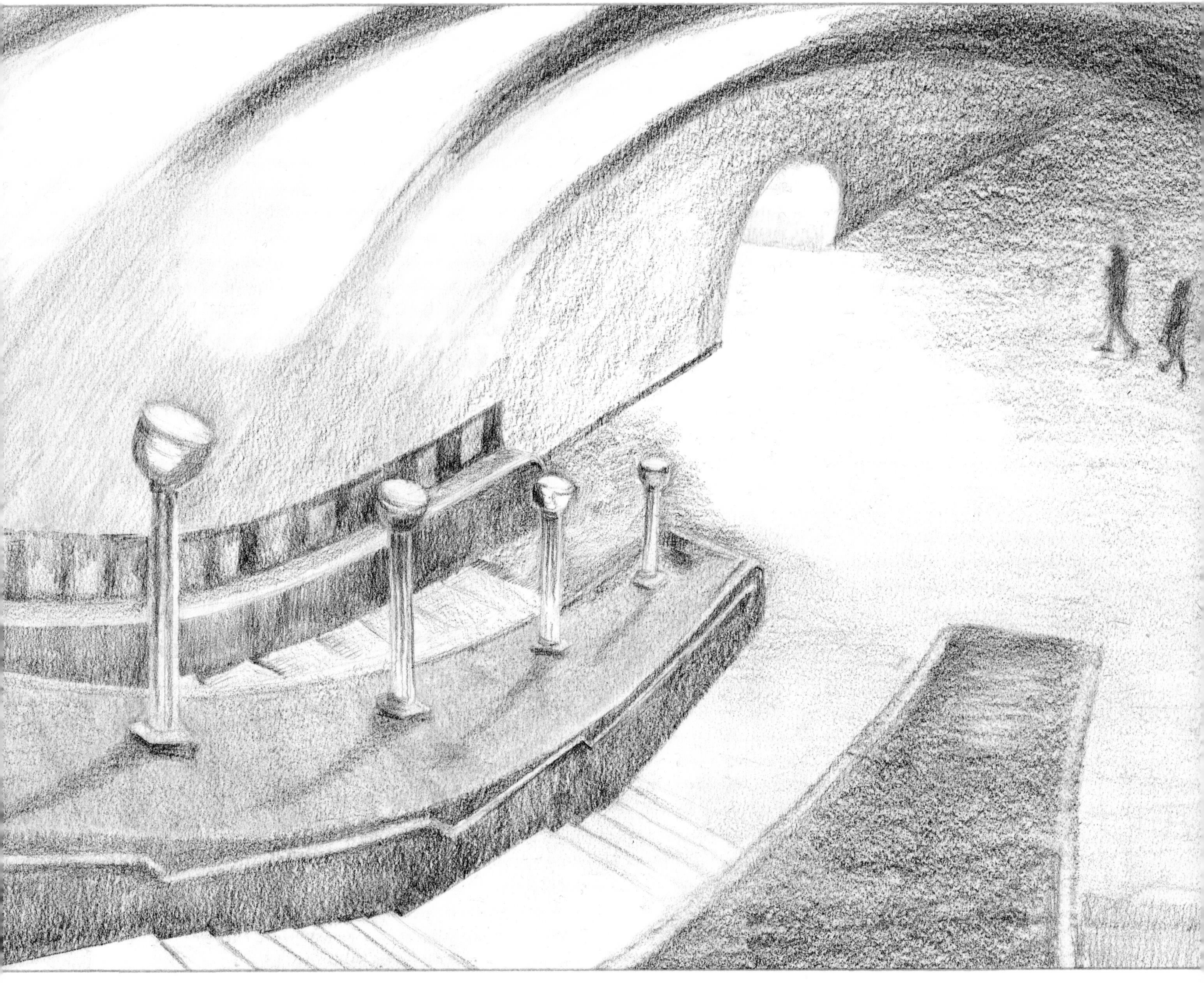

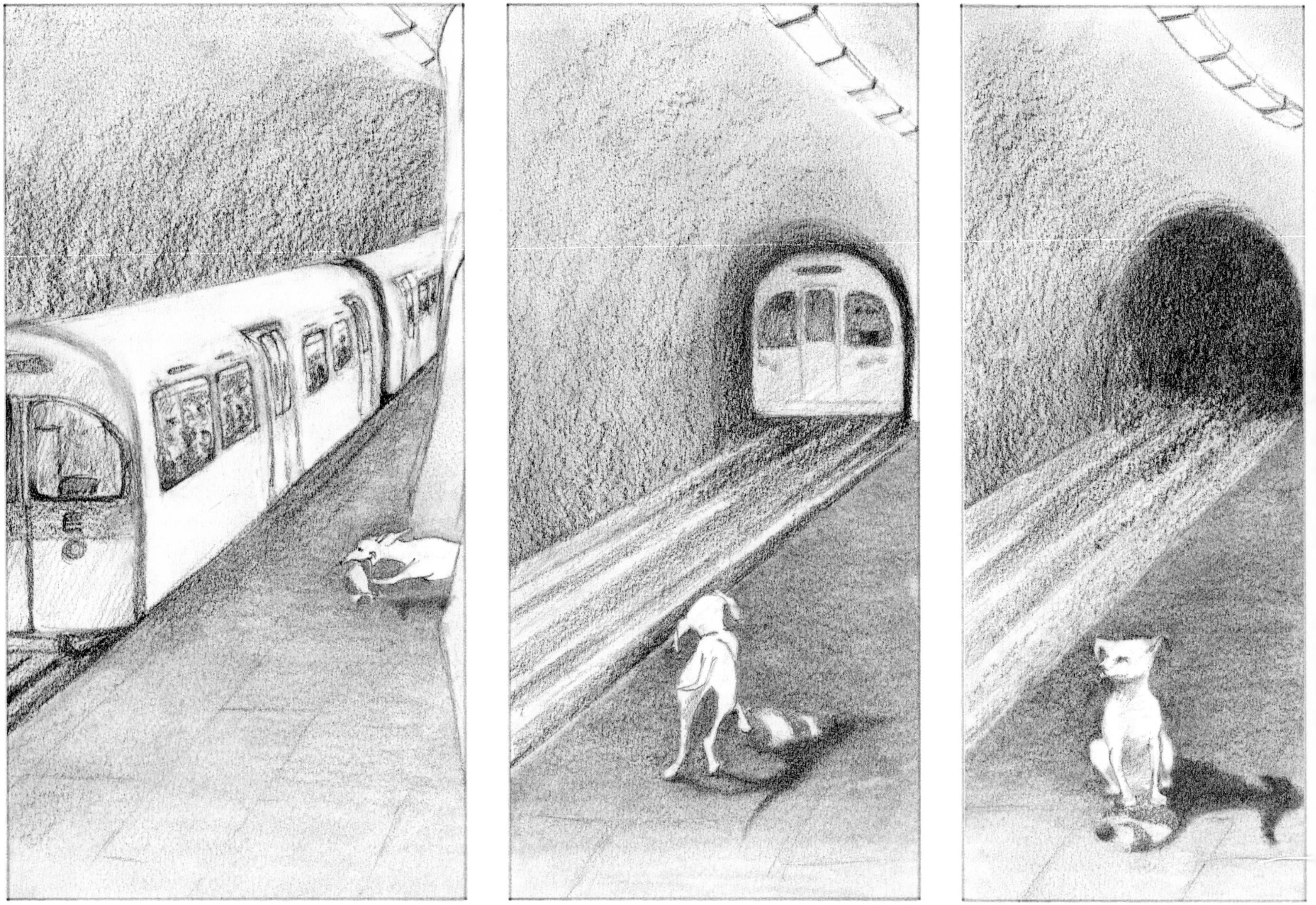

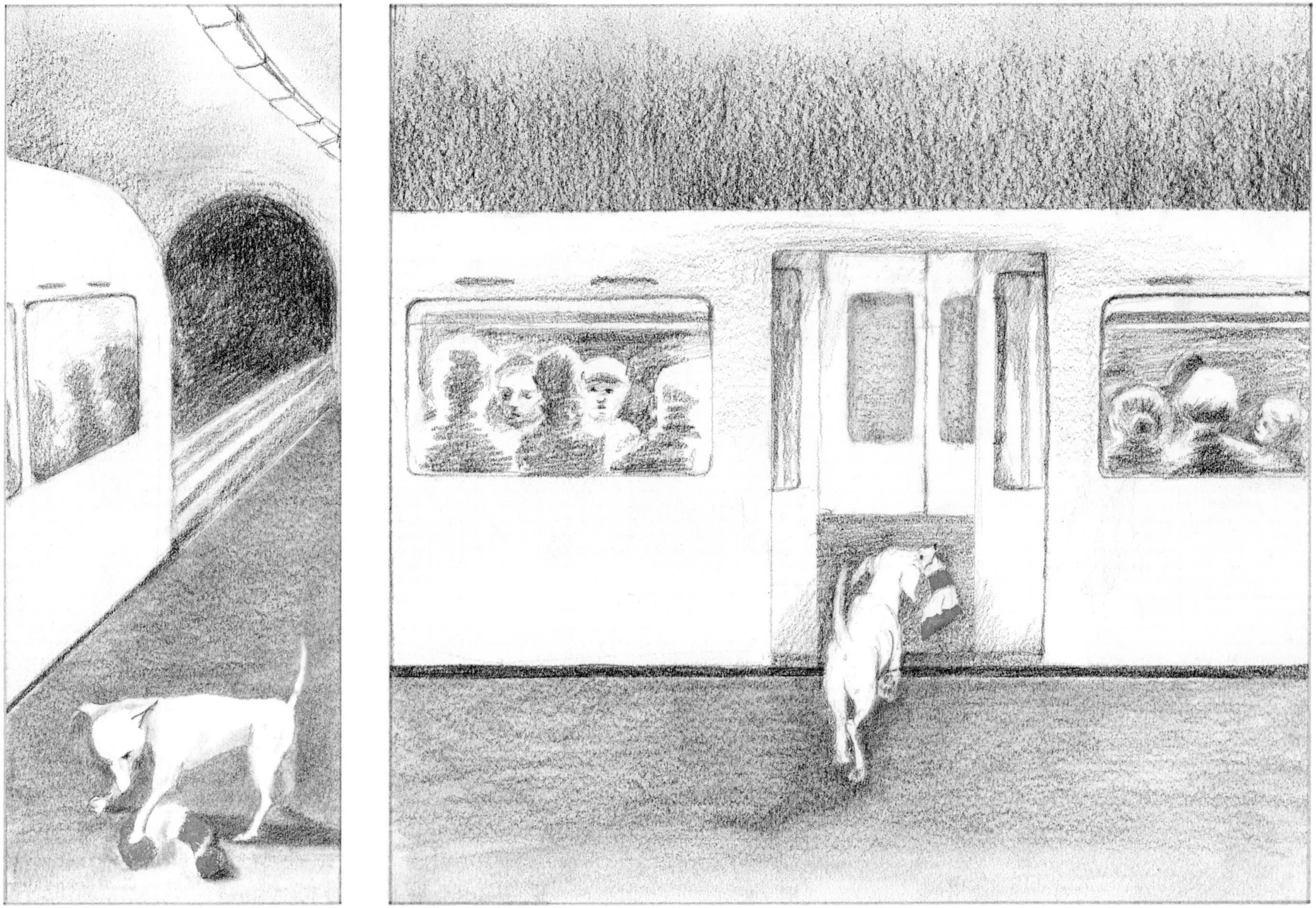

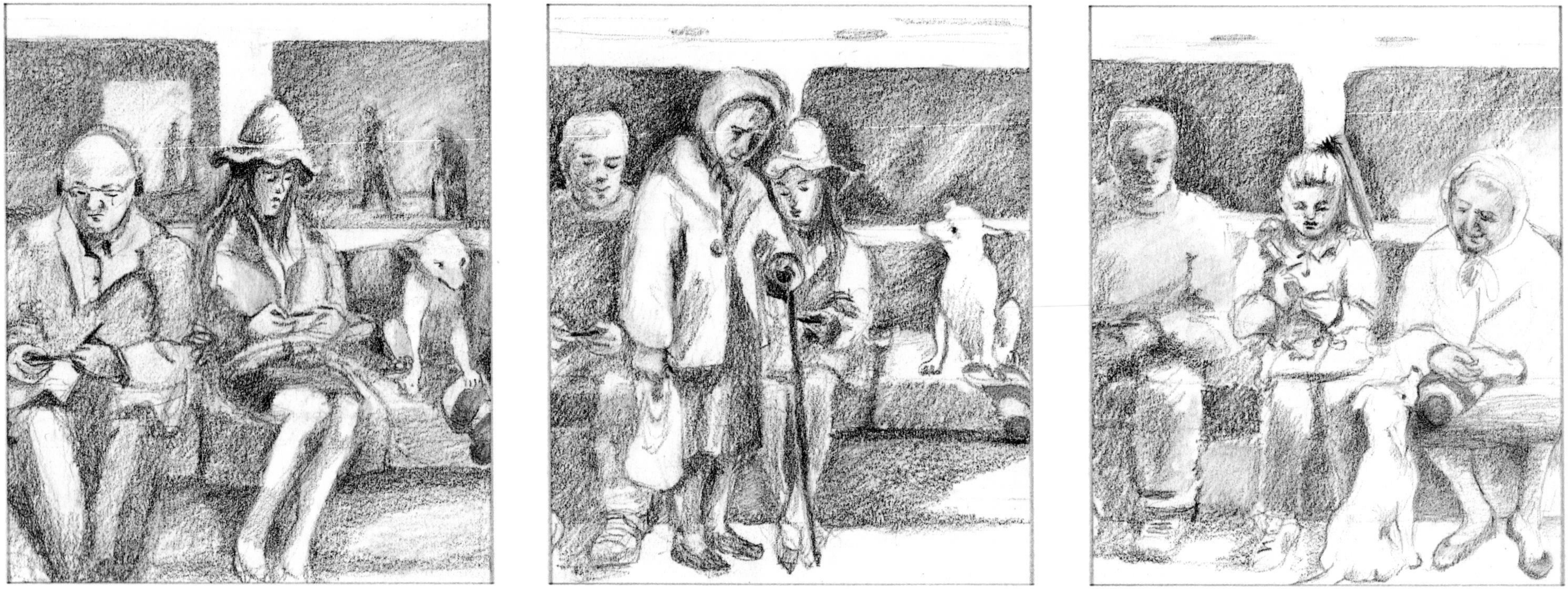

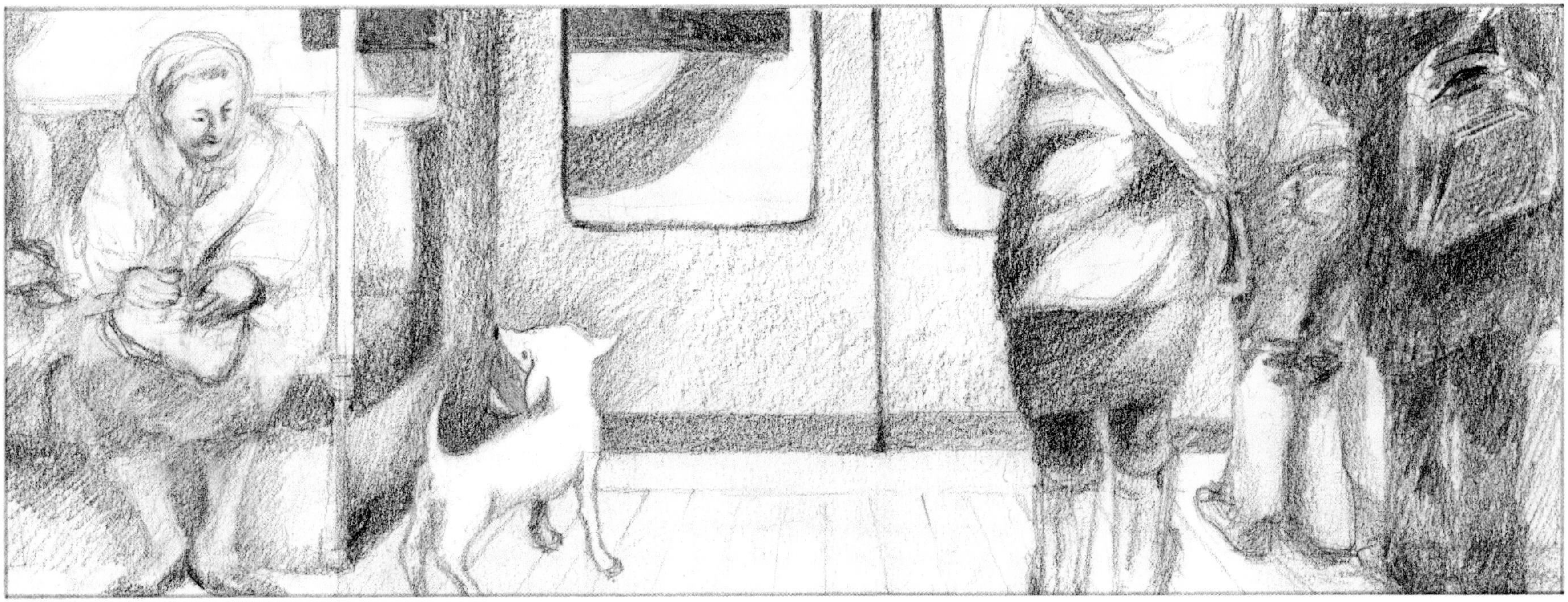

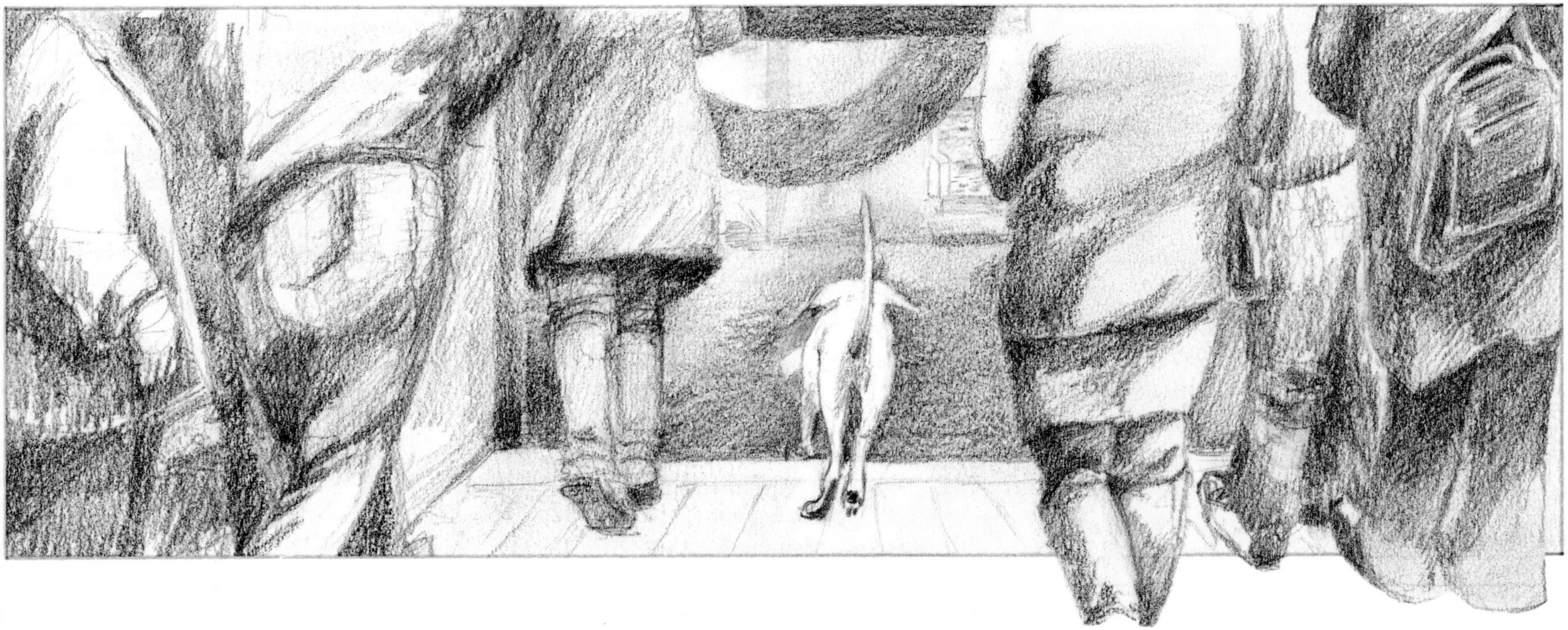

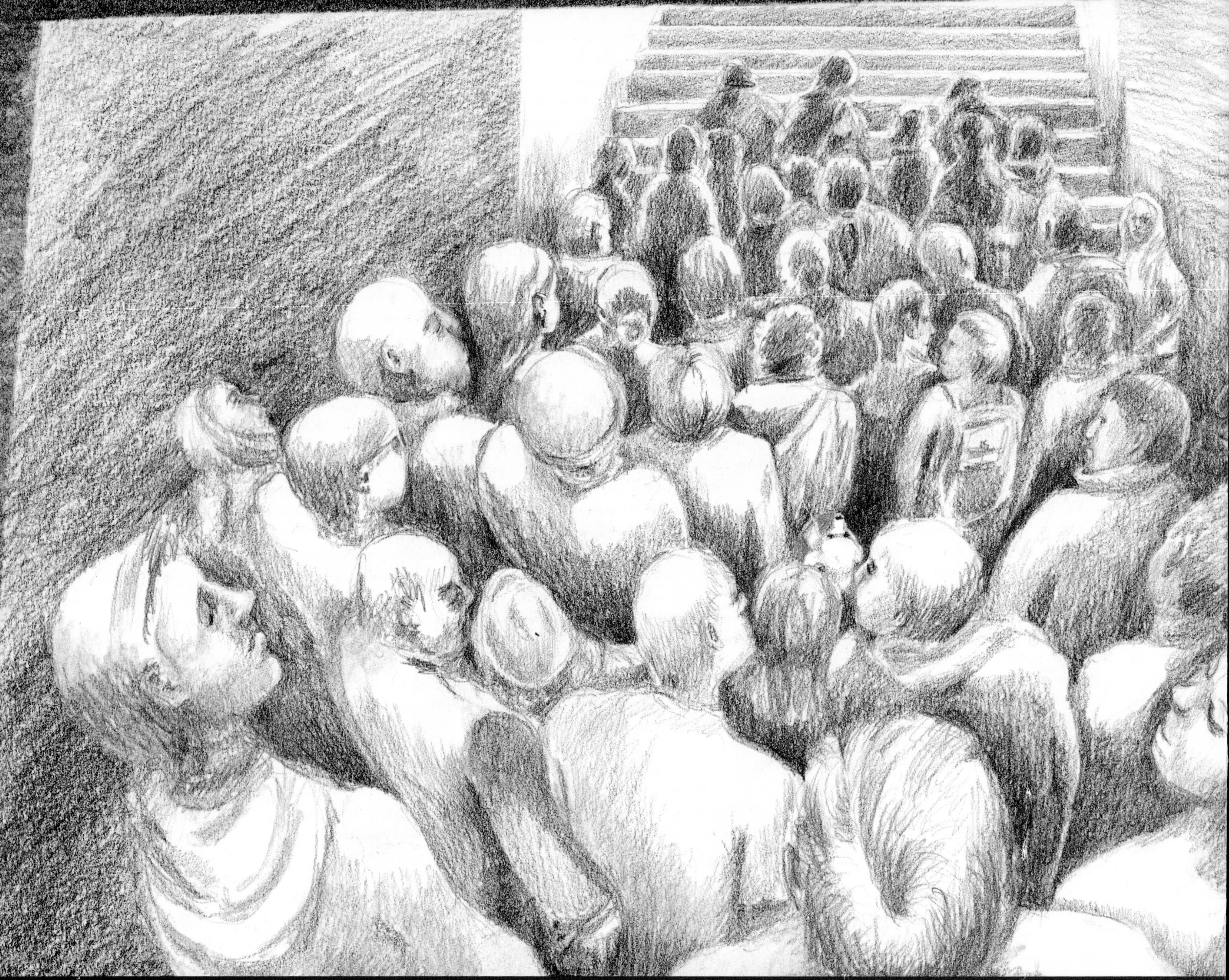

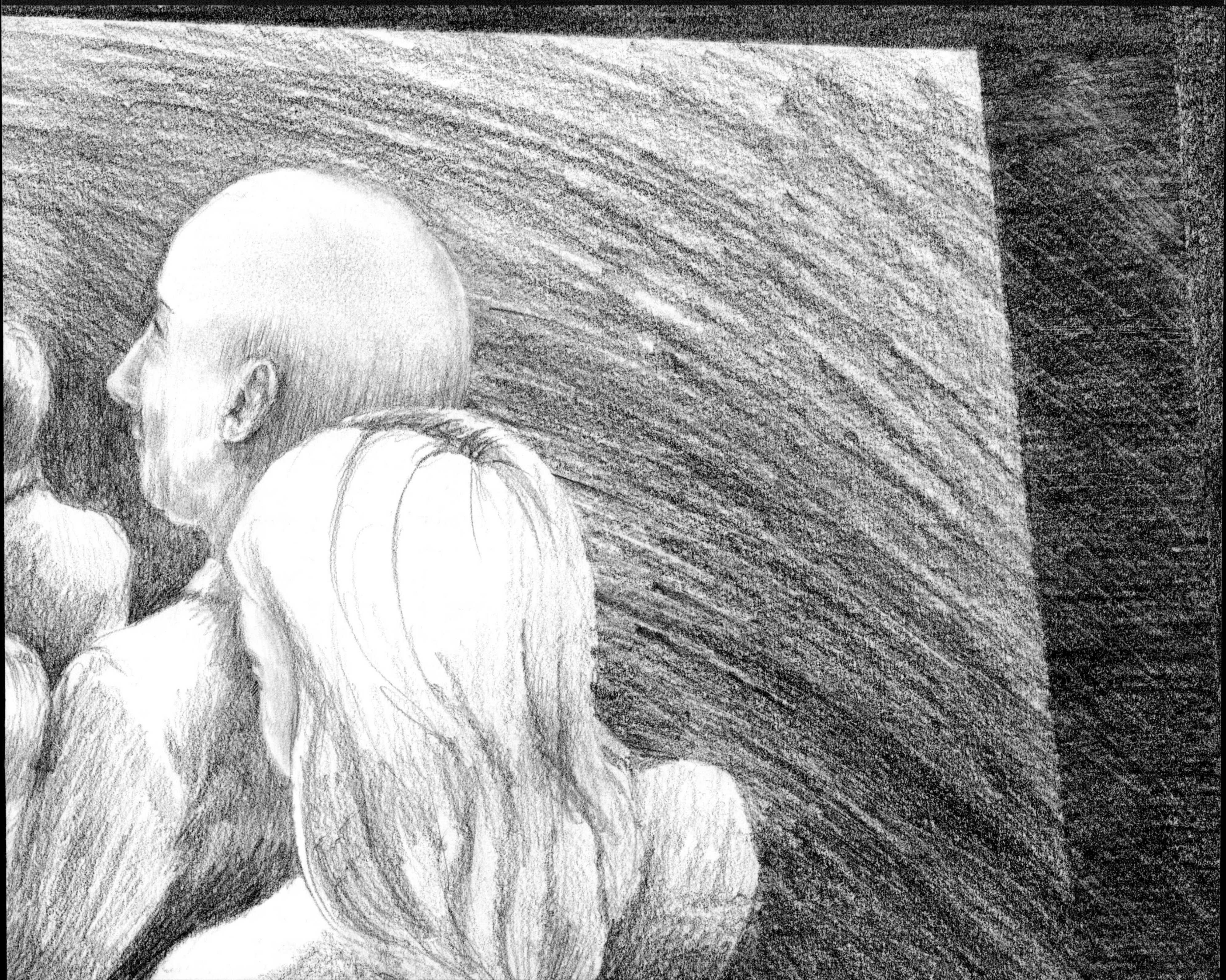

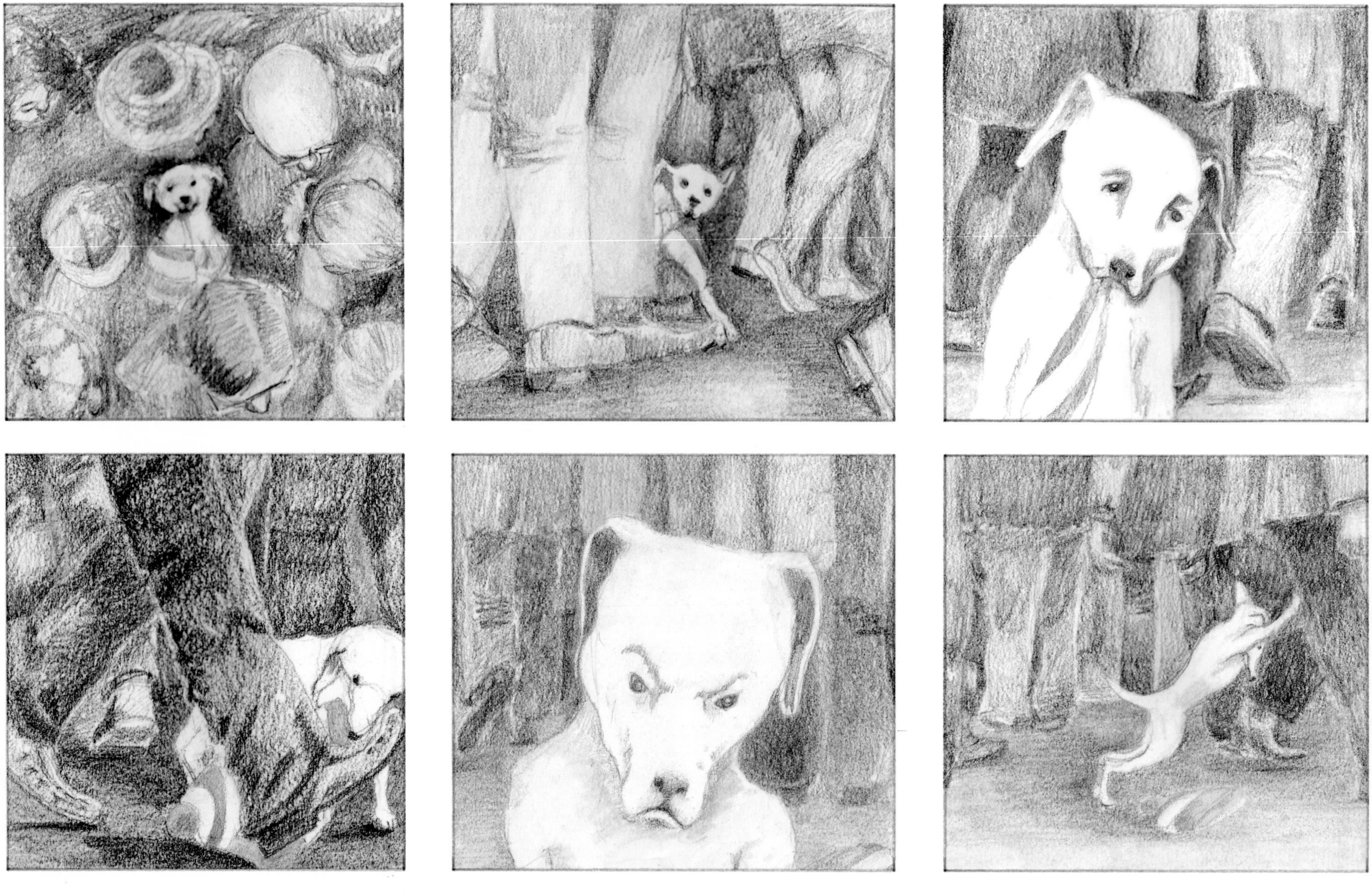

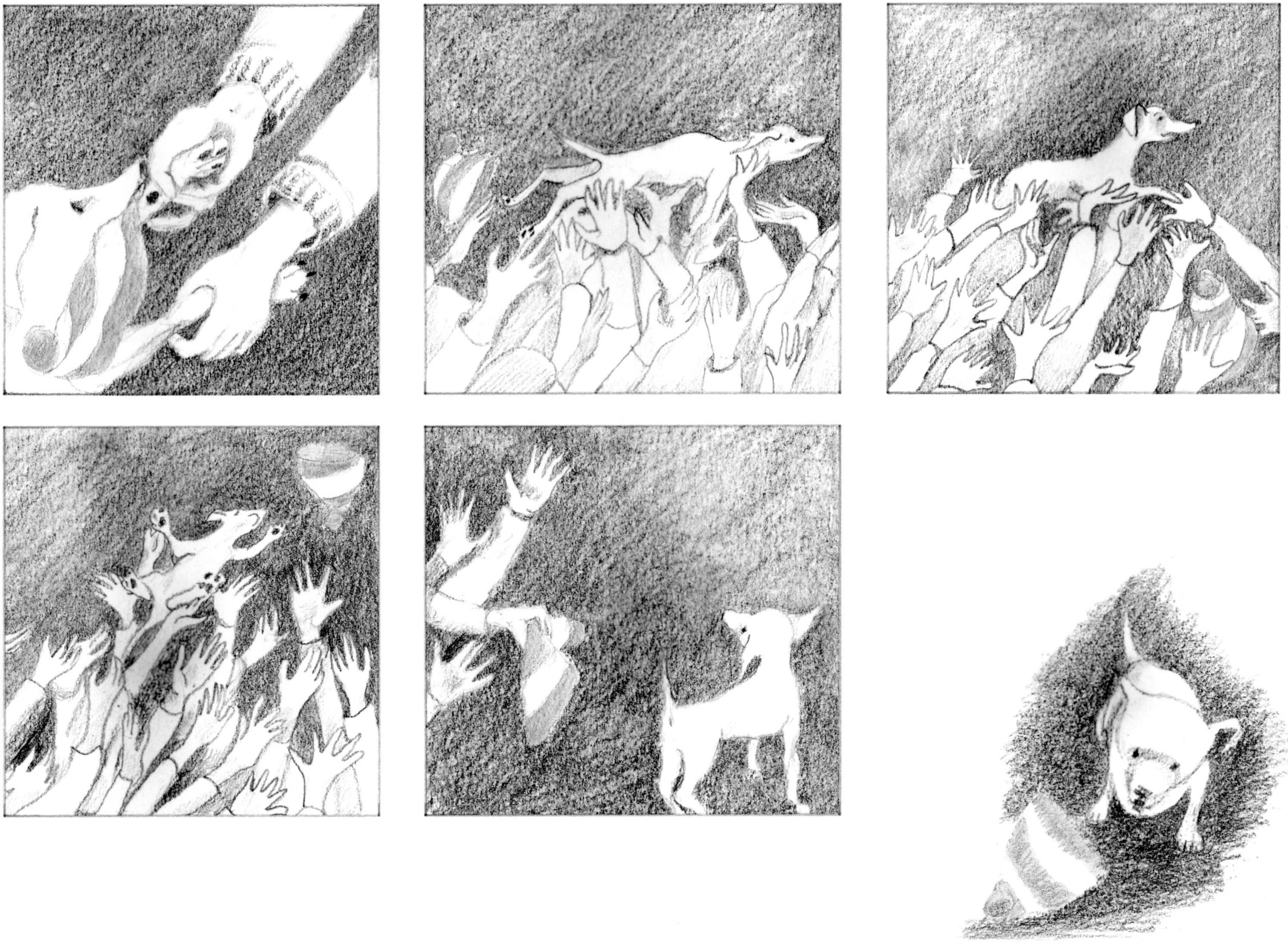

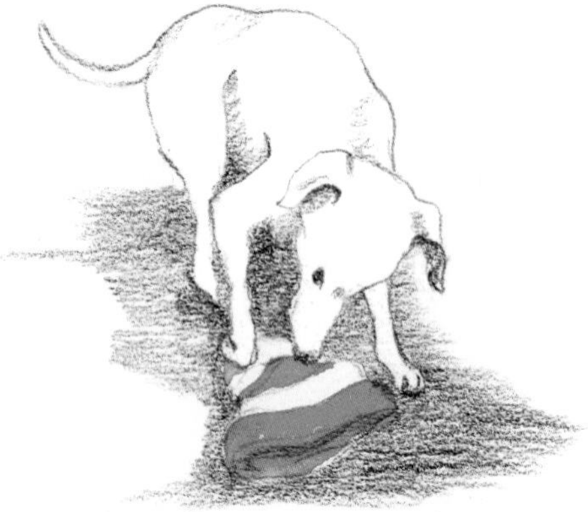

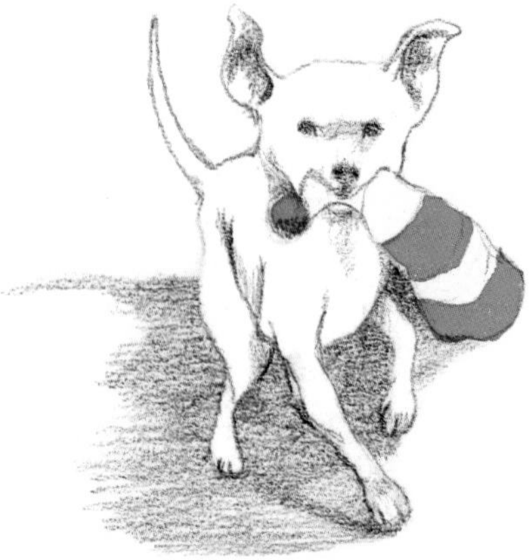

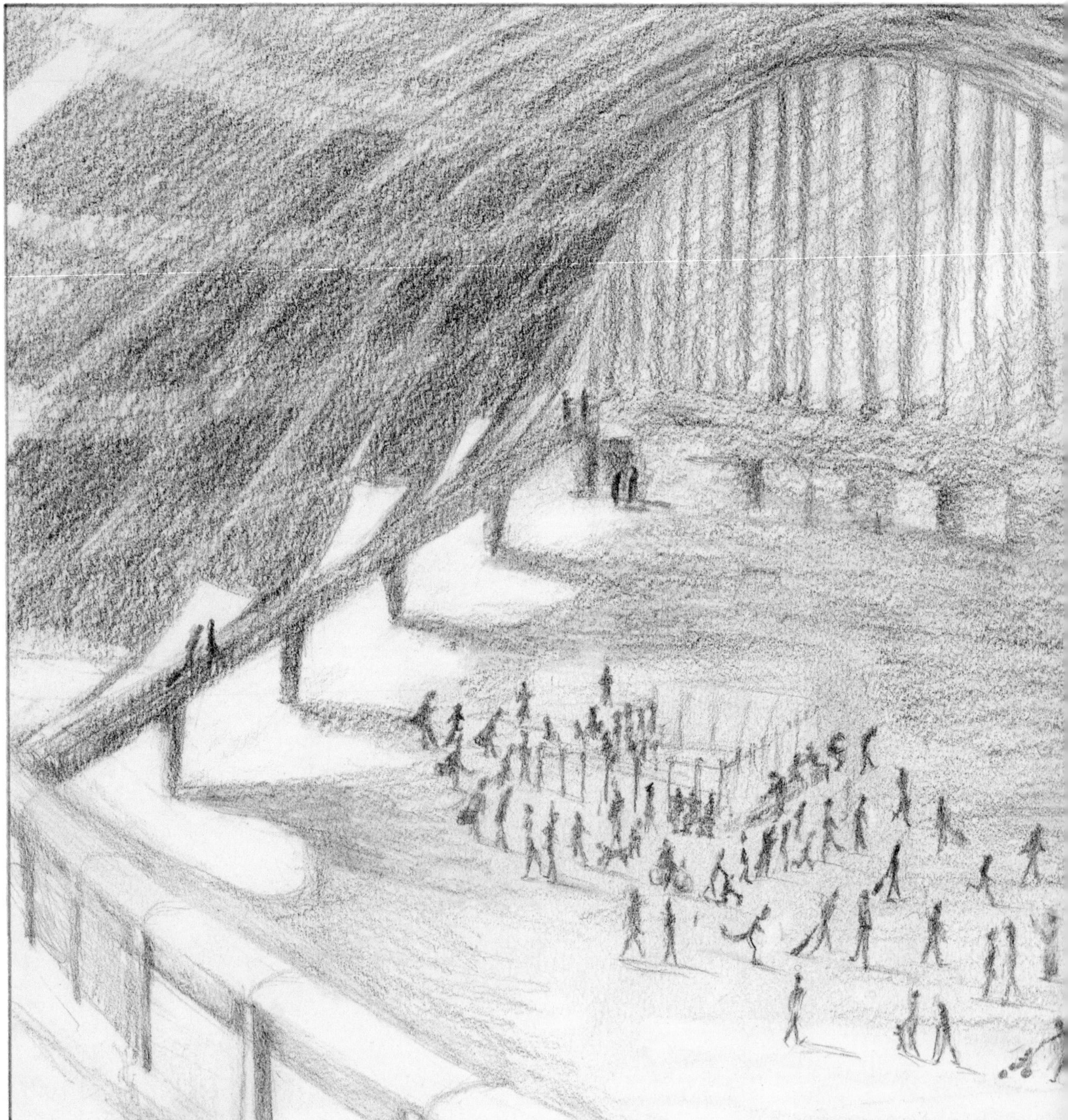

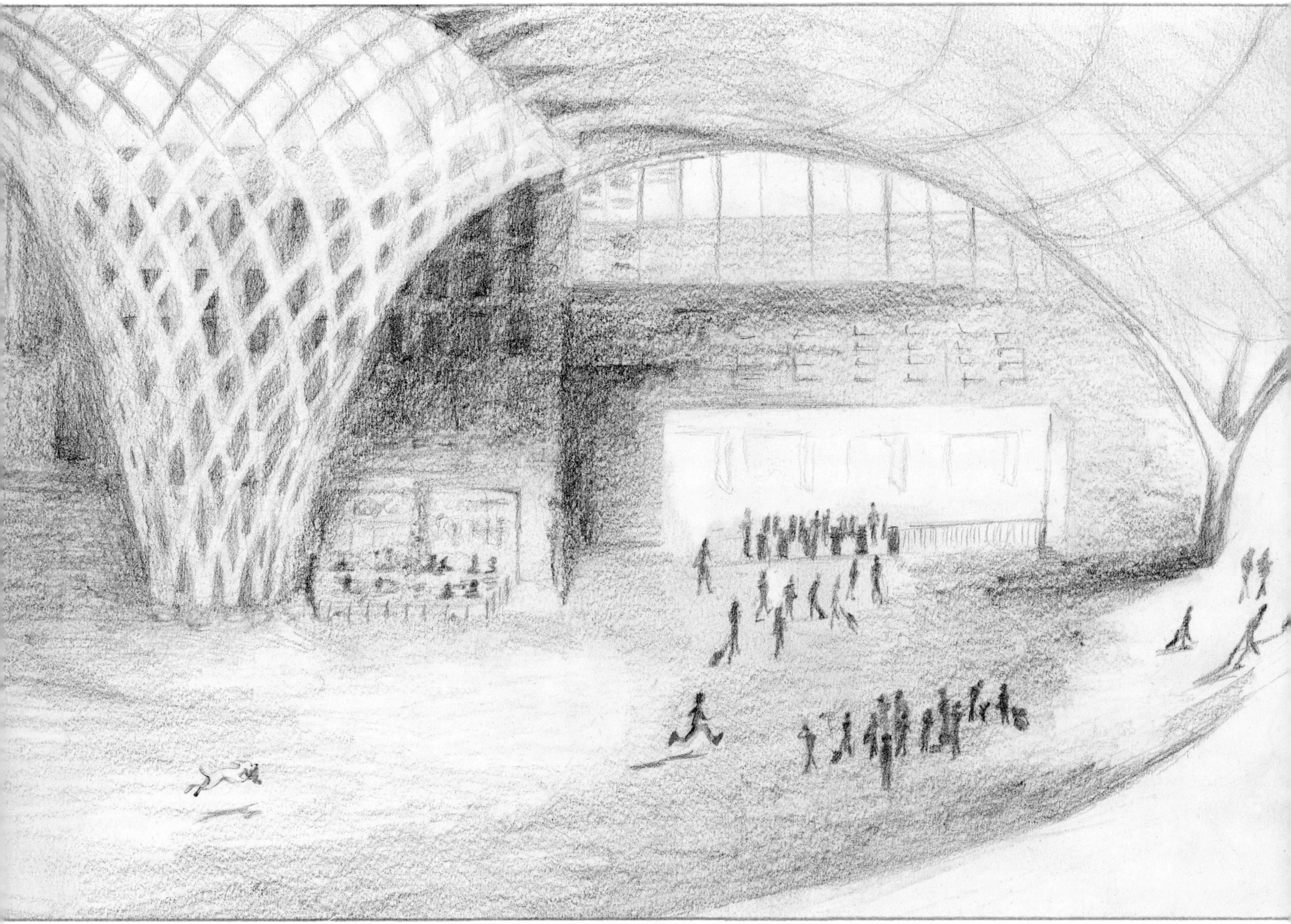

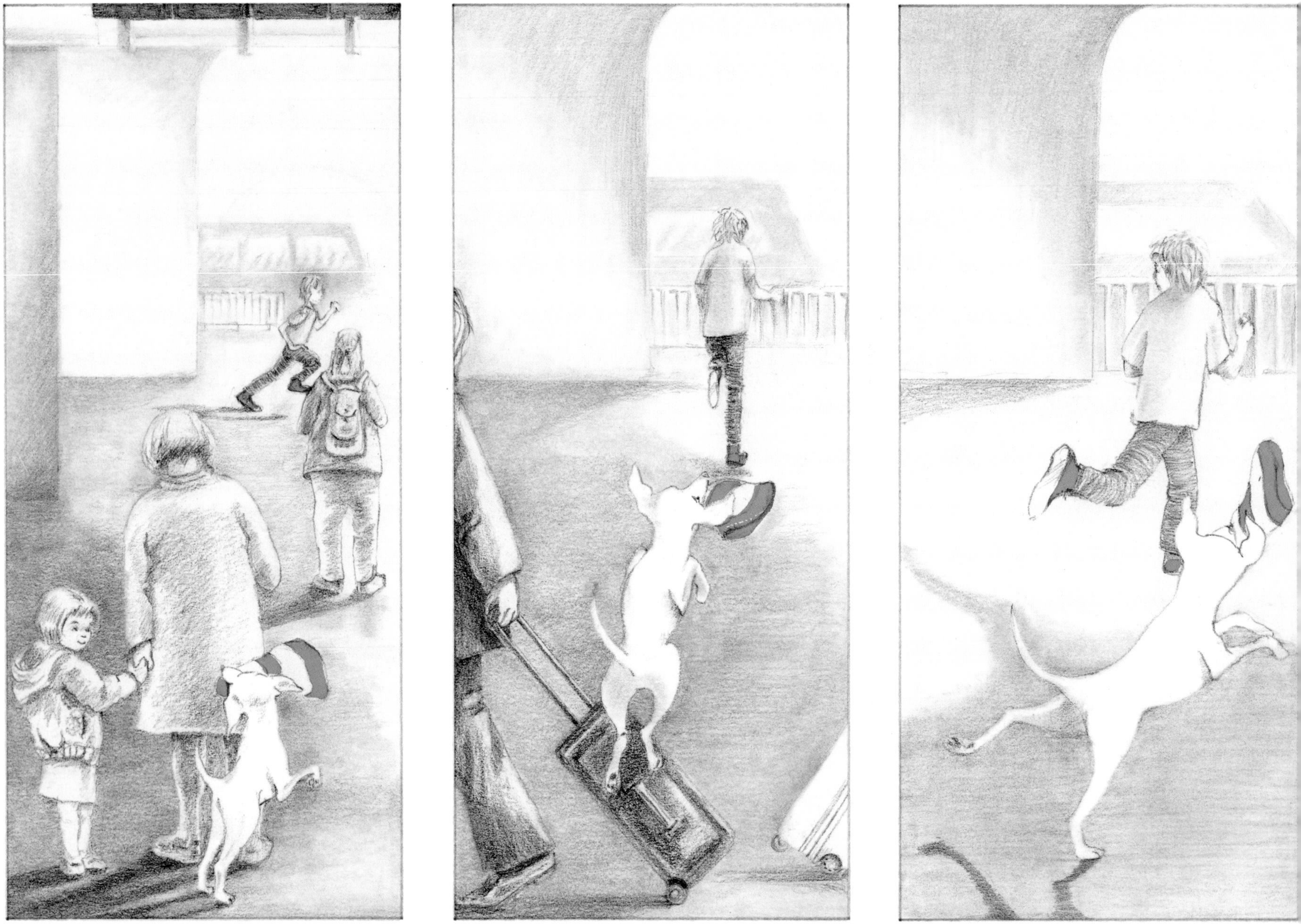

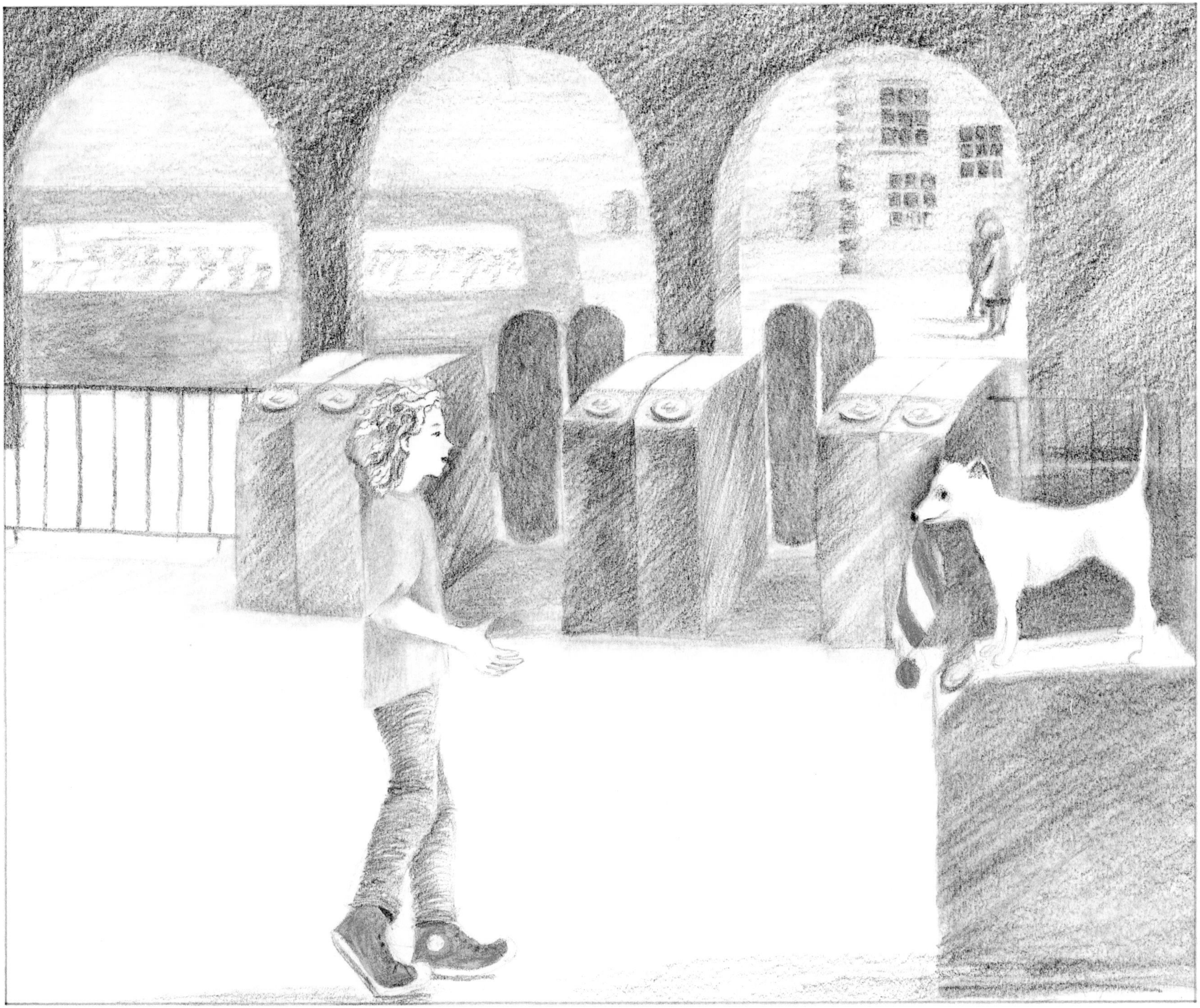

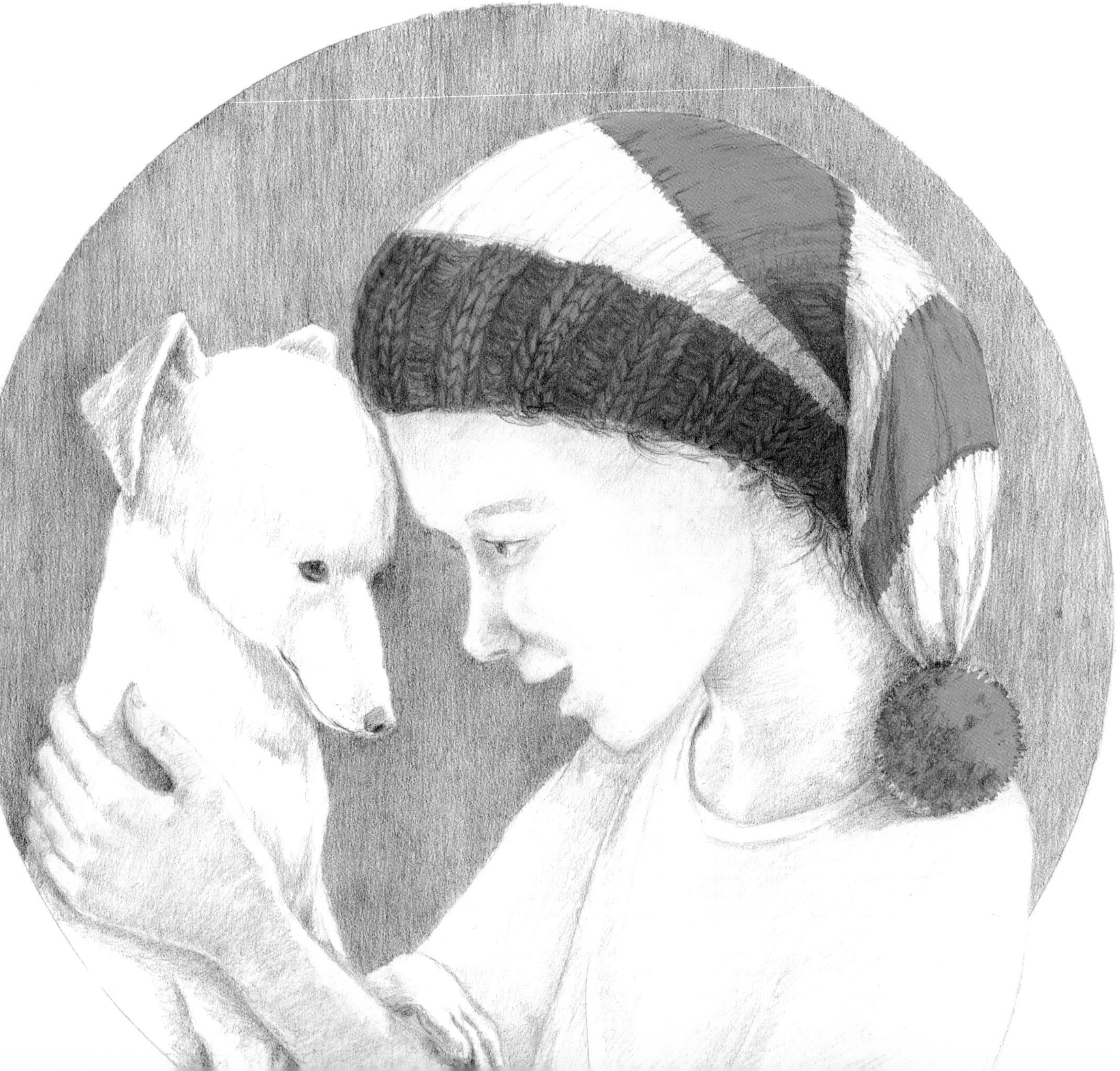

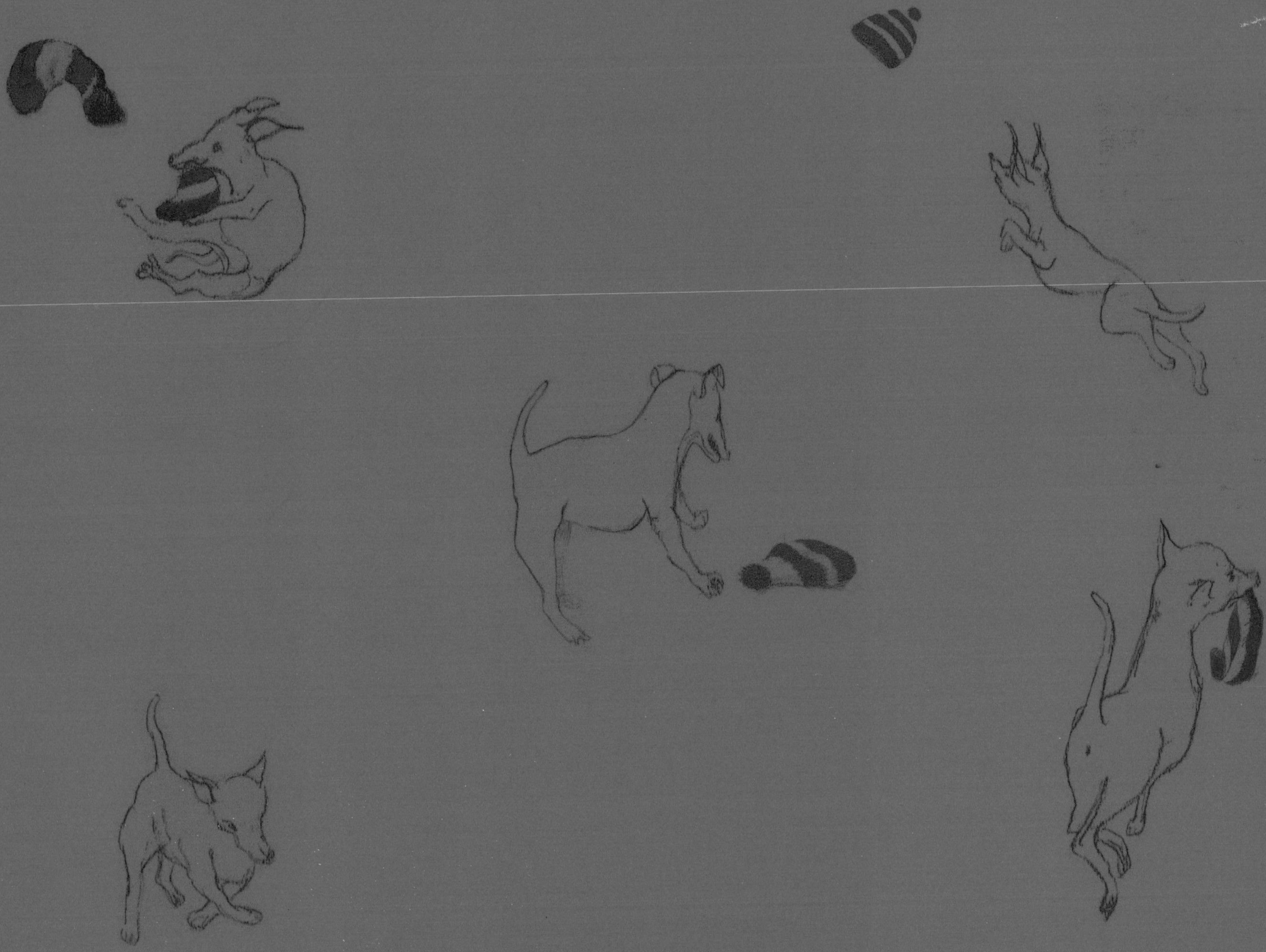